Drop Dead!

Billy Van Zandt and Jane Milmore

A SAMUEL FRENCH ACTING EDITION

SAMUELFRENCH.COM
SAMUELFRENCH-LONDON.CO.UK

ISBN 978-0-573-62839-9

www.SamuelFrench.com
www.SamuelFrench-London.co.uk

FOR PRODUCTION ENQUIRIES

UNITED STATES AND CANADA
Info@SamuelFrench.com
1-866-598-8449

UNITED KINGDOM AND EUROPE
Plays@SamuelFrench-London.co.uk
020-7255-4302

Each title is subject to availability from Samuel French, depending upon
country of performance. Please be aware that *DROP DEAD!* may not be
licensed by Samuel French in your territory. Professional and amateur
producers should contact the nearest Samuel French office or licensing
partner to verify availability.

MUSIC USE NOTE

Licensees are solely responsible for obtaining formal written permission from copyright owners to use copyrighted music in the performance of this play and are strongly cautioned to do so. If no such permission is obtained by the licensee, then the licensee must use only original music that the licensee owns and controls. Licensees are solely responsible and liable for all music clearances and shall indemnify the copyright owners of the play(s) and their licensing agent, Samuel French, against any costs, expenses, losses and liabilities arising from the use of music by licensees. Please contact the appropriate music licensing authority in your territory for the rights to any incidental music.

IMPORTANT BILLING AND CREDIT REQUIREMENTS

If you have obtained performance rights to this title, please refer to your licensing agreement for important billing and credit requirements.

DROP DEAD! opened Friday, May 31, 1985 at the Dam Site Theatre, Tinton Falls, New Jersey under the title *I Don't Want Her, You Cadaver (She's Too Stiff For Me)*. It was produced by Kathy Reed and directed by Billy VanZandt. Set design was by William Lee and Oaad Heulitt. Lighting design was by Joseph Rembisz. Costumes were by Russell Schiavone. Sound design was by Scott Wheeler. The Stage Managers were Neil Murphy and Jennifer Milmore. The cast (in order of appearance) was as follows:

PHILLIP	Glenn Kelman
CHAZ LOONEY	Glenn Jones
BRENT REYNOLDS	Jonathan D. Mack
CANDY APPLES	Jane Milmore
SOL WEISENHEIMER	Don Brennan
DICK SHALIT	Art Neill
VICTOR LE PEWE	Billy Van Zandt
MONA MONET	Sherle Tallent
CONSTANCE CRAWFORD	Kay Stansbury
ALABAMA MILLER	Jack Ryan

DROP DEAD! made its New York debut at the No Smoking Playhouse, Thursday November 6, 1985 produced by the Sherbet Organization in association with the Never-Never-Landers. Directed by Mr. Van ZandL Set design was by William Lee and Oaad Heulitt. lighting design was by Joseph Rembisz. Costumes were by Russell Schiavone. Sound design was by Scott Wheeler. The Stage Managers were Neil Murphy and Bob Hendrickson. The cast (in order of appearance) was as follows:

PHILLIP	Glenn Kelman
CHAZ LOONEY	Glenn Jones
BRENT REYNOLDS	Jonathan D. Mack
CANDY APPLES	Jane Milmore
SOL WEISENHEIMER	Don Brennan
DICK SHALIT	Don T. Gretzinger
VICTOR LE PEWE	Billy Van Zandt
MONA MONET	Sherle Tallent
CONSTANCE CRAWFORD	Kay Stansbury
ALABAMA MILLER	Denis Lynch

DROP DEAD! opened in Los Angeles at The Court Theatre on August 16, 1991. It was produced by Mitch Nedick and Edward P. Vogels. It was directed by Billy Van Zandt. Set design was by Robert W. Zentis. Lighting design was by Mike Pearce. Costumes were by Elizabeth Dirks. Sound design was by Scott Wheeler. The Stage Managers were Jennifer Milmore and Keith Cable. The cast (in order of appearance) was as follows:

PHILLIP . . . . .Glenn Kelman

CHAZ LOONEY. . . . . Craig Bierko

BRENT REYNOLDS. . . . . .Jonathan D. Mack

CANDY APPLES. . . . . Jane Milmore

SOL WEISENHEIMER . . . . .Barney Martin

DICK SHALIT . . . . Michael Kostroff

VICTOR LE PEWE. . . . . Billy Van Zandt

MONA MONET . . . . :. . . . . . . Adrienne Barbeau

CONSTANCE CRAWFORD . . . . Rose Marie

ALABAMA MILLER . . . . .Don Most

CHARACTERS

CHAZ LOONEY – The Apprentice Actor

CANDY APPLES – The Producer's Girlfriend

BRENT REYNOLDS – The Method Actor

DICK SCORSESE – Martin Scorsese's Cousin

MONA MONET – The TV Star

VICTOR LE PEWE – The Director

P.G. "PIGGY" BANKS – The Producer

PHILLIP – The Stage Manager

CONSTANCE CRAWFORD – The Legendary Stage Star

ALABAMA MILLER – The Playwright

ACT ONE

(Lights come up full on the drawing room of the Barrington Estate. We see a tuxedoed butler in a cutaway coat and white gloves dusting the painted-on fireplace. This is **CHAZ LOONEY** *playing the role of* **DROOLS** *the butler. He is much too young for the role and wears exaggerated bad age makeup. He speaks in an exaggerated English accent. He delivers all of his lines out front as if reciting in a children's pageant. He slyly uses crib sheets sewn inside his jacket and script pages, which are visibly taped underneath all his props.)*

DROOLS. Ah, what a sad day for the Barringtons. Especially Lord Barrington, who was found horribly murdered as he ate cheese in the library. Gouda cheese. Sliced thin.

(He peeks a look at his crib sheets and takes three steps to C.S.)

I have slaved for this family since I was a little boy, as my father did before me and his father before him, and my grandmother beside him, and my mother beneath her.

(The door chimes.)

Ah, the door is chiming. I must answer it, as I have done since I was a little boy, and as father did before me, and his father before him, and my grandmother beside him, and my mother beneath her.

*(***DROOLS*** walks to the front door, tripping on the rug – which is painted on the floor. He opens the door U.S.R. and we see* **BRENT REYNOLDS** *as* **ALEXANDER BARRINGTON,** *and* **CANDY APPLES** *as his new bride* **PENELOPE.***)*

(Sound effects: Raging Windstorm)

(A small burst of snow is thrown in after them as they enter. They wear coats. ALEXANDER wears a fedora. PENELOPE carries a small overnight bag. ALEXANDER and PENELOPE pose together D.S.C.)

Young Alexander Barrington.

ALEXANDER. Drools. Kindly Drools. Ever faithful. Ever true.

DROOLS. And who is the young woman I see before me?

ALEXANDER. Drools, I'd like you to meet my new bride, Pen-el-ope…

DROOLS. *(ad libbing)* Don't you mean, Penelope?

ALEXANDER. You're so right, Drools. I just call her "darling."

PENELOPE. A delight.

DROOLS. The delight is mine.

ALEXANDER. Ah, Drools. It's a sad day for the Barringtons.

DROOLS. May I take your coats?

(DROOLS takes their coats and Alexander's hat. ALEXANDER wears a smoking jacket and ascot underneath. DROOLS hangs their things on the coat rack. Since it is painted on the wall, they fall to the floor.)

ALEXANDER. Is mother about?

DROOLS. She's been under quite a strain. Finding the lord like that. Face down in the Gouda. Sliced thin.

ALEXANDER. *(posing dramatically)* Poor Mother.

PENELOPE. *(posed identically)* Poor thing.

ALEXANDER. How is she?

DROOLS. Hasn't touched a dairy product since.

ALEXANDER. And my sister…

(disgusted)

Bette…

(back to normal)

Has she arrived yet?

DROOLS. Yes, she's come, sir. Arrived this morning. Singing out loud like a little bird.

PENELOPE. How odd.

ALEXANDER. Not really. She has a beautiful voice.

DROOLS. I'll see if the Lady Barrington is up and around. May I take your suitcase?

(**PENELOPE** *holds out her suitcase, but* **DROOLS** *never takes it.*)

Please help yourself to the sherry. It will warm you from the winter chill. He exits up left.

(**DROOLS** *exits through the archway U.S.L.* **PENELOPE**, *unexpectedly stuck with a prop, hurls the suitcase offstage through the archway. We hear it smack* **CHAZ** *in the head. And a yell of pain.*)

CHAZ. *(off)* Ow.

PENELOPE. *(Spitting gum into her hand)*

There's a chill in the air. A chill about this house, Alexander. An evil chill. That I cannot explain. I am frightened. Hold me. Hold me.

(**PENELOPE** *and* **ALEXANDER** *embrace.* **CANDY**'s *gum sticks to* **ALEXANDER**'s *back.*)

ALEXANDER. *(trying to reach the gum on his back)* You're all right. As long as I'm around, Pen-el-ope.

PENELOPE. I feel better knowing that you are near.

ALEXANDER. I'll never leave you. Never.

(**ALEXANDER** *steps forward into a spotlight as the stage lights blackout.*)

The snow. Falling snow. White snow. Snow everywhere. Snow. Each flake different and unique in a…

(pronouncing the "ch")

…melancholy way. Yet together…a mass…of constant white…

(Spotlight off – stage lights up full as **ALEXANDER** *steps back into the scene. Snow falls outside the window*

– from a cheaply made "snow machine" hanging above the window.)

PENELOPE. What are you trying to tell me, Alexander?

*(**ALEXANDER** crosses to the fireplace. We see a big wad of pink gum stuck to his back. He picks up a poker, which he uses to poke the plastic fireplace log.)*

ALEXANDER. I was born and raised in this house, Pen-el-opp. I lived here my entire life. With the exception of school and college and day camp. And the week I was kidnapped by the man in the Blue Mask. This home is my blood. This home and…

*(Spotlight on – stage lights out as **ALEXANDER** steps forward.)*

… The Snow…

*(Spotlight off – stage lights up as **ALEXANDER** steps back into the scene.)*

(posing at fireplace)

There's nothing I wouldn't do to keep it. Nothing.

*(**DICK SCORSESE** as **INSPECTOR MOUNDS** enters from the archway. He wears a tweed Sherlock Holmes coat and cape, a Deerstalker hat, his Martin Scorsese glass frames, and smokes a large pipe.)*

INSPECTOR. "Anything?" What do you mean by "anything?")

*(**ALEXANDER** and **PENELOPE** exchange looks – never having said the word.)*

ALEXANDER. Who the hell are you?

*(**CANDY** begins mouthing all the other actors' lines.)*

INSPECTOR. Me?

ALEXANDER. Yes.

INSPECTOR. Inspector Mounds.

ALEXANDER. Beg your pardon?

*(**INSPECTOR MOUNDS** dramatically poses at the fireplace – with his foot set on the log.)*

INSPECTOR. Inspector Mounds. Scotland Yard. I'm investigating your late father's death.

ALEXANDER. And what have you found? We have nothing to hide here.

INSPECTOR. Nothing?

ALEXANDER. Nothing that can't be explained.

INSPECTOR. Explained?

ALEXANDER. And what else do you know, Inspector?

INSPECTOR. We know that your late father didn't die accidentally.

ALEXANDER. You mean…

INSPECTOR. Murderrr!

(Sound effects: Ominous Music Sting)

PENELOPE. Oh, Alexander. Hold me. Touch me. Thrill me.

*(Spotlight on – stage lights out, as **ALEXANDER** steps forward.)*

ALEXANDER. Looks like snow.

*(Spotlight off – stage lights up, as **ALEXANDER** steps back into the scene.)*

INSPECTOR. Would you mind answering some questions, Mr. Barrington?

ALEXANDER. I have nothing to hide.

INSPECTOR. The reading of the will will tell the tale.

ALEXANDER. Meaning?

INSPECTOR. Exactly what was your sister Bette's relationship with your late father?

*(**MONA MONET** sweeps in as **BETTE**. She glides in as she speaks, smoking from a long cigarette holder. She rehearses a grand bow for the audience's expected applause.)*

BETTE. Marvelous, Inspector. We got along divinely. I was like a daughter to him and he was like a father to me. I miss him so.

(flicking away a tear)

It's hard to believe he's really gone.

(**DROOLS** *pops in to deliver a punchline, carrying a tray with script pages taped to the bottom.*)

DROOLS. I say! He's not really gone. He's still in the study. They haven't come for the body yet. Snow and all.

(**DROOLS** *exits.*)

BETTE. Hello, brother.

ALEXANDER. Hello... Bette!

BETTE. You must be the new one.

ALEXANDER. Bette...this is Pe-nep-o-le. Pe-nep-o-le... Bette.

PENELOPE. Delighted. What did you mean, "New one?"

(**BETTE** *and* **ALEXANDER** *exchange looks.* **CANDY,** *the actress playing* **PENELOPE,** *continues mouthing the other actors' lines.*)

INSPECTOR. Yes. What did you mean? I didn't quite follow that myself.

BETTE. Didn't dear brother tell you? You're number thirteen. Unlucky number thirteen! Ha ha!

PENELOPE. Thirteen? Thirteen what?

BETTE. Why, thirteen wives, you little unsuspecting fool!

PENELOPE. Wives?

BETTE. Ha ha!

PENELOPE. I thought I was the first.

BETTE. Naive foolish petulant child!

ALEXANDER. You are the first, Pen-el-opp. The first that meant anything.

PENELOPE. Alexander...what happened to them? Were they pretty?

ALEXANDER. They were all lovely.

(*stepping forward*)

Especially Gwendolyn.

(*removing a paper from his pocket and reading it*)

"With her fair skin, tight sweaters, and massively large jugs."

PENELOPE. Where are they now?

ALEXANDER. She was buried with them.

PENELOPE. You mean...

ALEXANDER. Dead.

PENELOPE. You mean?

BETTE. Murderrr!

(Sound effects: Ominous Music Sting)

ALEXANDER. I always meant to tell you that, dear.

PENELOPE. Murdered? All of them?

ALEXANDER. Not at the same time. Individually.

INSPECTOR. Interesting, Mr. Barrington. If you'll excuse me.

(The INSPECTOR dramatically exits stage left face first into the painted-on archway. The slam sends chills up the other actors' spines. INSPECTOR slinks off through the archway, rubbing his face in pain. The other actors freeze until he is off.)

ALEXANDER. I was never convicted.

*(**INSPECTOR MOUNDS** screams from pain backstage.)*

BETTE. Ha ha. Juries can be bought. You never did explain that blood on your socks.

*(**DROOLS** enters through the archway with his tray/script.)*

DROOLS. Mr. Barrington, your mother can't wait to see you. I told her that you had arrived and her face lit up like a shining sun in the noon day...

(can't remember the line)

...sun. Presenting Lady Barrington!

(All pose, and NO ONE enters. There is an awkward pause.)

Presenting Lady Barrington... She cannot wait to see you, Mr. Barrington. Her face... Lady Barrington.

BETTE. Ha ha!

ALEXANDER. I can hear Mother coming now!

DROOLS. Presenting Lady Barrington!

(from out in the audience we hear:)

VICTOR. Where the hell is she?

ALEXANDER. I shall go and find her!

VICTOR. Wait! Stop it! Stop it! Where the hell is Miss Crawford for God's sake? Phillip!

(VICTOR LE PEWE rushes up on stage from the audience, his hands filled with notes. Work lights come up, as stage lights go out.)

ALEXANDER. Please Mr. Le Pewe. We're rehearsing.

VICTOR. Does anyone but me realize that we open tomorrow night? Phillip!

(PHILLIP rushes on. The actors break character – MONA and BRENT bitch to each other. CANDY puts more gum in her mouth, and blows bubbles. CHAZ LOONEY takes out a compact and adds yet another layer to his bad makeup. Between strokes of the brush, CHAZ flirts with CANDY. DICK SCORSESE enters from backstage reading a Police Gazette.)

PHILLIP. Yes Mr. Le Pewe?

VICTOR. Where the hell is Miss Crawford? We could have gone out for a sandwich here.

PHILLIP. *(exiting)* Miss Crawford!

BRENT. Why are we breaking?

VICTOR. Miss Crawford did not enter, in case you didn't notice, Mr. Observant.

BRENT. Miss Crawford never enters. She's stone deaf and can't hear the other actors, in case you didn't notice, Mr. Director.

MONA. I am tired of carrying her through this production, Victor. I was hired to play one role. Not two.

VICTOR. A little respect for Miss Crawford, please?

CHAZ. How does my makeup look?

VICTOR. Fine, Hiawatha.

VICTOR/PHILLIP. Miss Crawford! Miss Crawford! Lady Barrington!

(CONSTANCE CRAWFORD enters – stage star of the 1950s. She is always in her own world.)

CONSTANCE. Now? Is it me?

VICTOR. It's all right, Miss Crawford. If you can't hear the other actors, perhaps you could see them from back there. We can use a sight cue.

CONSTANCE. What?

VICTOR. I said perhaps we could use a sight cue.

CONSTANCE. I'm waiting for my cue, darling.

CHAZ. *(yelling)* Is this all right??

CONSTANCE. What?

VICTOR. *(to BRENT)* Do you think you could project a little?

BRENT. Mr. Le Pewe, I learned to project on a mountaintop, with pebbles in my mouth, reciting Shakespeare to the winds.

VICTOR. Sorry, Brent, we haven't got any winds here.

DICK. Yes, we do.

(motioning to CRAWFORD)

Stand behind her!

VICTOR. People, please! We haven't even gotten through the first half of the play! When you speak with Miss Crawford…just yell your brains out.

BRENT. I hardly think yelling my performance is the answer.

VICTOR. The answer is mercy-killing, but we're opening tomorrow.

CONSTANCE. Shall we take it from my entrance?

VICTOR. In just a minute!

(CRAWFORD shuffles off backstage anyway.)

Phillip! Perhaps we can push her out from the back?

PHILLIP. Yes, Mr. Le Pewe.

VICTOR. While we are stopped, may I give a few notes?

(**EVERYONE** *whips out their smart phone and checks messages, ignoring* **VICTOR** *as he reads his notes – all except for* **PHILLIP**, *who listens intently.* **PHILLIP** *catches the actors texting and quickly collects all the smart phones, before* **VICTOR** *notices.*)

(*reading from notes*)

"Muscatel the actors open!"

(*to* **PHILLIP**, *sotto voce*)

What the hell does this say?

PHILLIP. "Mouthing the actors again."

VICTOR. Yes. Candy…sweetheart…darling…you are mouthing the other actors' lines, again dear.

CANDY. I know.

VICTOR. I know, too. I saw it.

CANDY. That's how I learned my lines. I hear their lines in my head and then I know when to talk.

VICTOR. Do you think you might say their lines in your head with your mouth closed? Or shall I staple your lips shut?

CANDY. I'll say them in my head with my mouth closed.

VICTOR. I'm so glad.

(*reading notes*)

Miss Monet! If you insist on taking a bow every time you enter the stage, perhaps you shouldn't make your first entrance until curtain call.

MONA. Are you correcting me in front of the cast, dear?

VICTOR. I'm merely suggesting.

MONA. Face it, Le Pewe, when I enter, people will stand and applaud.

VICTOR. Darling, you haven't worked since your television series went off the air in 1997.

MONA. "Everyone Knows Mona" was top ten for two years. We beat the pants off "Dharma and Greg." Jenna Elfman still doesn't speak to me over it.

CANDY. Who?

BRENT. But this is theater, Mona. Applause must be earned by your years of dedication to the theater. Besides, if they're going to applaud for anyone, it will be for me.

MONA. Try saying Penelope three times fast.

BRENT. Mr. Le Pewe!

VICTOR. Mona! Brent! Please! We don't need this petty sniveling. I can't tell you how much we all need this. All of us. Mr. Banks has believed enough in our collective talents to bring this play to New York. Now perhaps it isn't Broadway…or even Off-Broadway… but it is theater!

MONA. There isn't even a sink backstage.

(**CANDY** *pops a bubble.*)

VICTOR. Miss Apples… Candy!

CANDY. Huh?

VICTOR. Please leave the gum offstage.

CANDY. It relaxes me to chew gum.

VICTOR. Little British ingenues don't chew gum. Little porno stars from Van Nuys chew gum.

CHAZ. Really Mr. Le Pewe. I don't think it's necessary to call Candy names.

VICTOR. I'm not calling her names, you asshole.

CANDY. What did he call me?

CHAZ. A British ingenue.

(**CANDY** *rushes to the edge of the stage.*)

CANDY. Piggy! Piggy! Daddy!

VICTOR. Oh, don't call Mr. Banks. I didn't mean it, Candy. The gum could work.

CANDY. Piggy! Mr. Le Pewe is upsetting me, Daddy!

DICK. "Daddy?" Mr. Banks is your father?

ALL. (*mumbled*) No.

DICK. Ah…

(*from down the aisle, we hear:*)

PIGGY. What the hell is going on this time, Le Pewe, you over-paid psychopath?

*(**PIGGY** walks up to the stage from the audience.)*

VICTOR. Nothing. Just a little directorial criticism, Mr. Banks. I was explaining to Miss Apples that little British ingenues just do not chew gum.

PIGGY. It's innovative. That's what I want. I want a different angle. Different angles are money in the bank. And that's what we're all here for, isn't it?

VICTOR. That's what you're here for, Piggy.

PIGGY. The name is P.G. Banks, Le Pewe. Let me tell you something. If it weren't for me, you'd still be in the booby hatch – twitching and drooling in a corner somewhere. If you want to insult people, start with the ham with all the Shakespeare training.

*(to **BRENT**)*

What the hell are you, a moron? The name is "Penelope." A moron can say that.

*(to **PHILLIP**)*

Say it.

PHILLIP. Penelope.

PIGGY. See? A moron can say it. What's your problem?

BRENT. It's one of those vicious blocks, Mr. Banks. A mental block.

VICTOR. A what?

BRENT. Nothing. Slip of the tongue. It'll pass, but for now I'm tripping over it.

PIGGY. Well, cut it out. You sound like a jackass.

BRENT. Yes sir.

VICTOR. Repeat after me. Pen.

BRENT. Pen.

VICTOR. El.

BRENT. El.

VICTOR. Ah.

BRENT. Ah.

VICTOR. Pee.

BRENT. Pee.

VICTOR. Pen-el-ah-pee.

BRENT. Pen-el-ah-pee-pee.

VICTOR. Fine.

MONA. Since we're stopped, I'd like to know what happened to Mr. Holst. He was good in the role.

(re: **DICK**)

This man, no offense, Dick, stinks!

PIGGY. Well, I didn't want to upset you, but Hal Holst was brutally murdered after rehearsal last night.

(All react with horror.)

It's okay. Luckily Mr. Scorsese here happened to be available.

(All sigh with relief.)

BRENT. "Available?" He's a TV repairman!

DICK. But I've seen quite a few plays with my cousin. I think I can do it as well as anyone. If you ask me, there's really nothing to it.

MONA. No one is asking you.

DICK. Well. That's what I think.

MONA. Oh, is that what you think... Dick?

VICTOR. And Dick's cousin... Martin Scorsese...will be coming to opening night.

(Pause.)

MONA. Welcome to the show, Dick. You are marvelous in the role. You really are.

CHAZ. Mr. Banks, I was thinking of using a French accent.

VICTOR. Mr. Looney. I've already told you "no." Quite emphatically.

PIGGY. French? I like it.

VICTOR. It's a British murder mystery.

PIGGY. So what?

VICTOR. Why would the butler be French?

PIGGY. France is right next door. He could be a commuter. He can wear a beret!

VICTOR. Mr. Banks… I was hired to direct this show. Need I remind you of my past laurels?

PIGGY. Need I remind you of your past fiasco? The one that put you in the booby hatch? The 200 million dollar bomb? The musical comedy story of the tsunami that destroyed Thailand? "Wave Goodbye to Daddy?" They flooded the audience with debris and little children's shoes.

VICTOR. I have directed some of Broadway's biggest successes! "Under the Veranda."

PHILLIP. "Life Beneath the Roses."

VICTOR. "Life Beneath the Roses."

PHILLIP. "Amarillo Galileo."

VICTOR. "Amarillo Galileo."

PIGGY. "Wave Goodbye to Daddy." Now, get in place and run this damn thing through. I have to take a whizz.

(**PIGGY** *exits through the audience, enroute to the men's room.* **CRAWFORD** *shuffles on.*)

CONSTANCE. I still can't hear you, dammit. Richard Burton always knew how to project!

VICTOR. I am Victor Le Pewe! Wonder Child of the Broadway Stage. No one talks to Le Pewe like that.

(**PHILLIP** *shoves some pills down* **VICTOR**'s *throat.*)

Okay, kids. Energy and pace. We'll take it from Lady Barrington's entrance.

CHAZ. Mr. Le Pewe?

VICTOR. Look, you little dildo, use a French dialect and I'll shove my foot up your accent.

PHILLIP. Ooh, any notes for me, Mr. Le Pewe?

VICTOR. Yes. Phillip. You must keep that snow machine working consistently. The entire message of the show just rests on the snow's consistency. Places! Dammit! We'll show them! This will be another Victor Le Pewe triumph!

(All move into position.)

Phillip, give me a place.

*(**PHILLIP** finds a spot in his manuscript.)*

PHILLIP. *(throwing himself into the role)* "Ha ha! Juries can be bought. You never did explain that blood on your socks." Bette.

MONA. I know my lines!

VICTOR. Action! Lights! Start dammit!

*(The actors get into position. **PHILLIP** drags off **CRAWFORD** when he exits backstage. Stage lights up – worklights out.)*

BETTE. Ha. Ha. Juries can be bought. You never did explain that blood all over your socks.

*(**DROOLS** enters from the archway, tray – script in hand.)*

DROOLS. Mr. Barrington, your mother can't wait to see you. I told her you had arrived and her face lit up like the shining sun…and everything. Presenting Lady Barrington.

*(Again, all pose dramatically. There is a pause. No one enters. **DROOLS** goes to the window and screams out.)*

DROOLS. Presenting Lady Barrington!

*(**LADY BARRINGTON** [**MISS CRAWFORD**] is pushed on through the archway by **PHILLIP**, who exits trying not to be seen.)*

CONSTANCE. I forgot where to stand.

*(**BRENT** points to a spot Stage Left. **CHAZ** pulls **CRAWFORD** over to her mark.)*

ALEXANDER. Mother! It's been so long!

LADY BARRINGTON. *(incorrectly addressing* **DROOLS***)* Alexander, my boy. You've come home!

CHAZ. Brent.

CONSTANCE. What?

CHAZ. *(pointing to* **BRENT***)* Brent!

LADY BARRINGTON. Brent, my boy. You've come home.

MONA. For Christ's Sake.

(**CHAZ** *tries turning* **LADY BARRINGTON** *to face* **BRENT.** *She continually turns back to face him.*)

LADY BARRINGTON. *(to* **DROOLS***)* I don't know how to tell you this son, but Daddy is dead. He died eating cheese. Gouda cheese. Sliced thin.

ALEXANDER. I know, Mother. That's why I've come.

(**CHAZ** *pushes* **CRAWFORD** *over to* **BRENT.***)*

LADY BARRINGTON. What is this?

ALEXANDER. My new bride, Mother. Pen-la-pee-pee.

(**CHAZ** *taps* **CRAWFORD** *to speak.*)

LADY BARRINGTON. Such a pretty child. So young. So sad. How old are you, my child?

PENELOPE. Twenty-three and one half.

(**CHAZ** *taps Crawford.*)

LADY BARRINGTON. Pity.

BETTE. *(to* **PENELOPE***)* If you knew what was good for you, you'd take the first train out of here.

(**CHAZ** *taps Crawford.*)

LADY BARRINGTON. It's too late. That was the last train leaving the station.

(Sound effects: Train Whistle.)

VICTOR. Good one, Phillip.

(**PHILLIP** *appears in the window and silently apologizes, and exits.*)

DROOLS. The trains are not running. Because of the snow.

(A clump of snow falls outside the window.)

We're all trapped here. Like rats in a pack.

(A piece of white cardboard grows up the window. It is snow trapping them inside the house. Pushed up by **PHILLIP**.*)*

LADY BARRINGTON. What does it matter? She's in the family now. There is no escape from her fate. Your fate is sealed, my dear.

*(***LADY BARRINGTON*** points to the window, and the cardboard snow.* **ALEXANDER** *steps forward, as spotlight goes on.)*

ALEXANDER. Especially in this snow…

(General stage lights come back up, and we see **INSPECTOR MOUNDS** *making shadow puppets in the spotlight.)*

BETTE. Inspector Mounds!

CONSTANCE. What?

BETTE. *(ignoring* **CRAWFORD***)* You're still here?

INSPECTOR. And so are we all. I'm glad I have you all here. I have found conclusive evidence which will point conclusively to the killer of Lord Barrington.

(All gasp. **CRAWFORD** *gasps two beats late.)*

Please, be seated.

*(***EVERYONE*** looks around panic-stricken. There is no place to sit. The chairs are painted on the walls. They all dive at the loveseat, Center-Stage.* **BETTE, PENELOPE,** *and* **CRAWFORD** *sit.* **ALEXANDER** *and* **DROOLS** *are forced to sit on the chairs painted on the walls. They sit trying to retain a shred of dignity. They fail.)*

The murderer is someone in this room!

(All gasp. **CRAWFORD** *gasps two beats late.)*

I found these two items on the body of the lord. Buried in the Gouda. Sliced thin. This letter!!…

(He whips out a letter. All gasp. **CRAWFORD** *gasps two beats late.)*

And this brassiere!

*(***INSPECTOR*** *pulls a big white bra out of his jacket. All "OOH.")*

*(***CRAWFORD*** *"OOH"s two beats late.)*

The contents of this letter, written in the murderer's own hand...

(All but **CRAWFORD** *look at their hands.)*

Together with this brassiere, monogrammed in the murderer's own initials...

(All feel their shirts. **CRAWFORD** *inspects her hands.)*

...conclusively conclude that the murderer is none other than...

*(***INSPECTOR*** *pauses, waiting for the stage lights to blackout on cue. As the* **INSPECTOR** *looks up to the stage lights, the lights)*

(Blackout.)

ALEXANDER. The lights!

BETTE. What's happened to the lights?

ALEXANDER. Somebody get the lights!

CANDY. Hey! Take your hands off me, you dirty pig!

BRENT. Sorry. Thought that was the light switch.

PENELOPE. Ah!!

CONSTANCE. My God, I've gone blind! I've gone blind!

DROOLS. Rutabaga. Rutabaga. Rhubarb. Rhubarb...

(Finally, the lights come up full. **ALEXANDER** *is nowhere near the light switch. He slowly edges his way to the switch trying not to be noticed.* **PENELOPE**'s *dress has been torn off, revealing a sexy corset and stockings.* **DROOLS** *is in* **BETTE**'s *arms.* **CRAWFORD** *is faced upstage, disoriented.* **INSPECTOR MOUNDS** *quickly places a plastic dagger under his arm and dies very dramatically Center Stage.*

As he dies, he accidentally drops the dagger. He quickly places the dagger back under his arm and dies on the floor. All gasp. Except **CRAWFORD** *who is now completely out of it.* **ALEXANDER** *dashes over to the* **INSPECTOR***'s dead body to take his pulse.)*

ALEXANDER. Good God. He's dead!

(The **INSPECTOR** *raises his arm.* **ALEXANDER** *reacts and takes the pulse.)*

PENELOPE. You mean…

(Everyone waits for **CRAWFORD** *to deliver her line. She merely stands facing the wall.)*

CHAZ. "Murder."

CONSTANCE. What?

CHAZ. "Murder!"

CONSTANCE. Is it me?

PHILLIP. "Murder!"

CONSTANCE. I'm sorry. I'm lost, Mr. Le Pewe!

VICTOR. "Murder!"

CONSTANCE. Does anyone know the line?

ALL. "Murder!"

CONSTANCE. Let me check the script.

*(***CRAWFORD** *exits backstage.* **ALABAMA MILLER** *dashes onstage from the audience. He wears rumpled shirt and pants, a raggedy cardigan sweater, a loose tie, and horn-rimmed glasses. His hair is wild. He carries a 576 page manuscript. He is wild with rage.)*

ALABAMA. What the hell do you people think you're doing?

VICTOR. Get him out of here, Phillip! This is a non-stop dress rehearsal, dammit!

(Work lights come up as **PHILLIP** *enters from backstage.)*

ALABAMA. Why is Penelope dressed like that?

VICTOR. How did you get in here?

ALABAMA. What the hell kind of a set is this?

*(re: **BRENT**)*

This man is sitting on the painting of a chair!

(**BRENT** *rises, trying to regain some dignity.*)

This play was written for black curtains and music stands.

VICTOR. Look, everyone. The playwright is here. Alabama Miller, I don't believe you know everyone...

ALABAMA. What have you done to my play? A lifetime of torment...bearing my soul...and you've slashed the guts out of it!

CHAZ. *(innocent)* When did you get out of the rehab center, Mr. Miller?

MONA. Clam up, Looney.

ALABAMA. *(re: **CANDY**)* Why is she dressed like that? Choir robes! Everyone in this play should be wearing choir robes!

VICTOR. Look, Alabama...if there's one thing I know how to mount, it's a show! Now, I have taken your soul, as you so nicely put it, and I have embellished it with the style only a Victor Le Pewe could give it. Now it is not only a dramatic triumph, now it is a commercial triumph as well. People will take one look at this show and say, "Le Pewe! Le Pewe!"

CANDY. I represent "women's repression and a new sexual freedom." Is that right, Mr. Le Pewe?

VICTOR. Yes. Yes. That is a statement that was just screaming to be made.

PHILLIP. Besides, Mr. Banks says T & A will goose the box office.

VICTOR. There comes a time, Mr. Miller, when it is best to just "go with the flow."

ALABAMA. "Go with the flow?" My play was 576 pages. Now it's 18 pages. And that includes the prop list.

PHILLIP. Yes, but now we can do three shows a night.

ALABAMA. You even changed my title.

VICTOR. "Drop Dead" is a catchy title.

ALABAMA. It's not my title. "The World Condition and the Eternal Snow God." That's the title. It sums up the whole point.

CANDY. I don't get it. It just sounds stupid.

(PIGGY *enters from the audience, zipping up his fly.*)

PIGGY. What's he doing here? I left word not to let you in.

(PIGGY *walks on stage, to* ALABAMA, *warm and friendly.*)

How are you feeling, Alabama? There's a bottle of scotch in my office. Go help yourself.

(ALABAMA *starts to sweat, thinking about the scotch.* PIGGY *goes to* CANDY.)

Doesn't she look great? Turn around, baby. I tell you, these bits I inserted make this whole show work.

(CANDY *shakes her tail.*)

BRENT. About that line you added, Mr. Banks...about the massively large jugs...

ALABAMA. What "massively large jugs?" What line? You can't do that!

PIGGY. Why not? You got the Inspector pulling out a bra.

ALABAMA. The bra represents human sexuality.

BRENT. And the snow?

ALABAMA. The eternal seasons of life. People facing the same battles generation after generation. The same snow that touched the earth during the time of Christ touches us now. It is a common denominator.

BRENT. Good. That's how I was playing it.

ALABAMA. The dead body onstage is the ever-present specter of death that looms over us all.

DICK. I don't see that.

PIGGY. I don't either. That can't be right.

ALABAMA. It can't be right? I wrote the play!

PIGGY. Cheer up. How many playwrights never even get produced. Huh? You didn't think of that, did you, Mr. Miller?

ALABAMA. I'll kill you. I'll kill you.

VICTOR. Get in line.

PIGGY. *(to* **PHILLIP***)* If I hear Alabama Miller interrupting my rehearsal again, I want you to throw him out of the theater. Got it, piss boy?

PHILLIP. Yessir.

(An enormous sandbag falls from the rafters, smashing to the ground inches away from **PIGGY** *and* **MONA***. AD LIB COMMOTION.* **VICTOR** *and* **PHILLIP***, and* **CANDY** *and* **CHAZ** *go to each other.* **PIGGY** *stares up into the rafters, as* **DICK** *inspects the sandbag.)*

PIGGY. Who's up there? Who's up there?

PHILLIP. There's nobody up there.

MONA. My God. I was almost killed. Doesn't anyone care about me?

(No one answers.)

Well?

VICTOR. *(rolling his eyes)* Are you all right, Mona?

MONA. If I didn't know better…if I weren't so loved by us all… I'd swear that sandbag was deliberately dropped to kill me.

PIGGY. Who would want to kill you? No one even remembers you.

DICK. This rope was cut!

MONA. First Hal Holst and now me!

CHAZ. We should call the police.

PIGGY. No police! I'm not insured.

ALL. What?

PIGGY. I mean… I'm not that sure… It was a silly little accident. It's over with.

MONA. I was almost killed. Call the police or I'm calling my agent!

VICTOR. Over my dead body. Nothing is going to interfere with this show opening tomorrow. Do you hear me? Nothing!

DICK. Can we get going here? Some of us have to get up and go to work for a living.

PIGGY. Mr. Scorsese is right. Places, please.

VICTOR. I'm supposed to say that. Places, please!

CHAZ. But gee…

MONA. Thank you all for being so understanding.

VICTOR. Take it from…what's the line, Phillip?

   (**CRAWFORD** *enters, pointing to a line in her script.*)

CONSTANCE. "Murder!"

   (**PHILLIP** *shoots* **CRAWFORD** *a jealous look and exits taking* **CRAWFORD**'s *script and the sandbag with him.*)

   (*Stage lights up – work lights out.*)

BETTE. Well, we know it's not Inspector Mounds.

LADY BARRINGTON. Then it must be someone in this room.

   (*All look suspiciously at each other.* **BETTE** *looks up into the rafters.*)

PENELOPE. I feel faint.

ALEXANDER. You should lie down, Penelipuss.

   (*He punches the wall.*)

I'll take you off to rest. Where shall we go to rest, Drools?

DROOLS. Any place but the study. It's occupied.

   (*The dead* **INSPECTOR** *sneezes.*)

ALEXANDER. Mother, will you be all right?

BETTE. With you gone, at least she'll be alive!

ALEXANDER. Why you dirty bitch!

   (**ALEX** *slaps* **BETTE** *theatrically.*)

BETTE. The truth always hurts.

ALEXANDER. I'll be back, Mother. Stay alive until I do.

LADY BARRINGTON. I will son, I will.

   (**ALEXANDER** *and* **PENELOPE** *exit through archway.*)

BETTE. A drink for Lady Barrington, Drools.

DROOLS. I live to serve you.

(**DROOLS** *exits, humbly bowing and groveling, smacking into the archway frame as he exits.*)

LADY BARRINGTON. I guess this leaves us quite alone.

BETTE. Quite.

LADY BARRINGTON. (*Stepping all over the dead inspector*) And I suppose we'll never know what Inspector Mounds was going to tell us.

BETTE. And I suppose that pleases you just fine, Mother, doesn't it?

(**BETTE** *crosses away.*)

LADY BARRINGTON. Why do you say that, Bette?

BETTE. You don't think I know, do you, Mother? About you blackmailing Daddy with those horrid photographs of him and the brownie troop earning special merit badges in the woods.

LADY BARRINGTON. So what, you horrid girl. And won't you be surprised to learn that you were cut out of your father's will and his entire estate was left to me. Me alone.

(**DROOLS** *enters with a goblet on a tray.*)

DROOLS. The drinks, mum. Shaken by hand.

(*He shakes his hand and exits.* **CRAWFORD** *speaks to where he stood before he left.*)

LADY BARRINGTON. Thank you, Drools.

BETTE. You think everyone's your servant, don't you Mother? You pompous, money-hungry, society bitch!

(**BETTE** *slaps* **LADY BARRINGTON** *with a bad, weak theatrical slap.*)

VICTOR. Stop it! Hold your places!

BRENT. (*popping his head in*) Can't we please go on without stopping?

*(Work lights go on – stage lights go out. **CRAWFORD** continues acting unaware they've stopped the rehearsal.)*

LADY BARRINGTON. You should have said that sooner, Bette…and won't you be surprised to learn—

VICTOR. We've stopped for a sec, Miss…we've stopped! We've stopped! We've stopped for a sec, Miss Crawford! Miss Monet, you have the most pathetic stage slap I've ever laid eyes on.

MONA. I don't do stunts.

VICTOR. Slap her.

MONA. Victor, I'm afraid of hurting her. She's ancient.

VICTOR. A proper stage slap does not hurt the actor. You should know that. Phillip! Come out here!

*(**PHILLIP** enters, script in hand.)*

PHILLIP. Yes, Mr. Le Pewe?

*(**VICTOR** slaps **PHILLIP** with such force his script and clipboard fly into the audience.)*

VICTOR. There. That didn't hurt. Did it, Phillip?

PHILLIP. Not at all, Mr. Le Pewe.

*(**PHILLIP** gathers his script up off the floor.)*

VICTOR. *(to **MONA**)* There. See? The meat of the neck cushions the blow and you may slap away to your heart's content.

*(**VICTOR** slaps **PHILLIP** again. This time **PHILLIP** really gets excited.)*

PHILLIP. Oh, Mr. Le Pewe…

VICTOR. Now, might we go on with our little opus before my hair turns white and I look like Anderson Cooper, for God's Sake?

MONA. Fine. You correct me in front of the cast again, and I walk.

VICTOR. No one walks out on Victor Le Pewe.

(to All) Take it from…

PHILLIP. *(sexy)* The slap.

VICTOR. Take it from…

> *(his eyes meeting* **PHILLIP***'s)*

…the slap.

> **(VICTOR** *and* **PHILLIP** *inhale and exhale together, in lust.* **PHILLIP** *exits.)*

Places!

> **(VICTOR** *exits into audience. Work lights go out as the stage lights come up full.)*

BETTE. You think everyone's your servant, don't you?

CONSTANCE. What?

MONA. We've started.

CONSTANCE. What?

MONA. We've started.

CONSTANCE. Have we started?

BETTE. You pompous, money-hungry…

CONSTANCE. Shall we take it from my entrance again?

BETTE. I've started. I'm acting! I'm attempting to perform!

CONSTANCE. Am I in the right spot? Sorry, but Mr. Le Pewe, these young actors of yours just move all over the place with no respect for your blocking.

MONA. *(to* **VICTOR***)* I'm in the same spot I've always been in.

> *(to* **CONSTANCE,** *as* **BETTE***)*

You think everyone's your servant, don't you?

CONSTANCE. Shall we begin?

BETTE. You pompous, money-hungry, senile, society bitch!

> **(MONA** *belts* **CRAWFORD** *in the jaw knocking her offstage. We hear awful crashing noises backstage, as well as* **PHILLIP***'s high-pitched squeal and* **CRAWFORD***'s low moans of pain.)*

MONA. Oh!

> *(Pause.)*

(to **VICTOR***)*

Was that better?

(VICTOR *moves forward, concerned.)*

VICTOR. Is she alive?

(PHILLIP *enters from backstage, in tears, bent over.)*

PHILLIP. Yes. She's fine. But Victor… I hurt my privates.

(VICTOR *is concerned.* **PHILLIP** *motions that he'll be all right.* **VICTOR** *is relieved.)*

VICTOR. Keep going.

(PHILLIP *exits backstage and pushes out* **CRAWFORD** *who has no idea what went on.)*

LADY BARRINGTON. You should have done that sooner, Bette. Now I see you as you really are. When I die, I'll see to it you're cut out of my will just as you were cut out of your father's massive inheritance.

BETTE. Before you do, here's your drink.

(BETTE *crosses to the bar and pours powder from her ring into the goblet on the tray. It bubbles.* **ALEXANDER** *enters through the archway with a white bed sheet.)*

ALEXANDER. I've brought a sheet for Inspector Mounds. It's off your bed…

(Spitting in **CRAWFORD** *'s eye)*

… Bette.

BETTE. White. How appropriate.

(ALEXANDER *covers the* **INSPECTOR** *with the sheet.* **DICK** *coughs from the dust. Mother takes the drink from* **BETTE***.)*

LADY BARRINGTON. *(toasting)* Cheers!

(She drinks.)

The lights. The lights are dimming. Drools, don't forget to pick up some new bulbs! The room is spinning. I can't catch my breath. The lights are fading. The lights are out!

(**LADY BARRINGTON** *dies on the love seat, Center Stage.*
CRAWFORD's *dress gets hiked up as she dies, and she lies
on the loveseat spread-eagle, revealing bright bloomers.*)

ALEXANDER. What are you trying to say, Mother?

BETTE. She said it tastes delicious.

ALEXANDER. *(taking her pulse)* Good God. She's dead.

(**CRAWFORD** *coughs.* **BRENT** *closes the gap in*
CRAWFORD's *legs. They continually fall back open.*)

BETTE. Nonsense. She's just sleeping. Wine tires her so.

(**MONA** *closes* **CRAWFORD**'s *legs. They fall back open.*)

ALEXANDER. How wrong you are, Bette. Unless I miss my
mark, her hot toddy has been spiked with a lethal dose
of…

(sniffs goblet)

…arsenic. I happen to be an amateur botanist.

(**BRENT** *and* **MONA** *close the gap in* **CRAWFORD**'s *legs.
They fall open again.*)

BETTE. Seems open and shut.

ALEXANDER. Yes, but to be safe I shall call for the police.

(**ALEXANDER** *heads for the telephone. As he reaches to
close* **CRAWFORD**'s *legs, she beats him to it and closes
them herself.* **ALEXANDER** *picks up the telephone at the
bar.*)

The telephone is dead! Father is dead! Mother is dead!
Inspector Mounds is dead! And now…the telephone.

(Sound effects: The Telephone Rings.)

(It is ignored by the actors. **PHILLIP** *appears at the
window and silently apologizes to the cast.* **ALEXANDER**
picks up a straw from the telephone table.)

This is the last straw. I refuse to stand by and watched
us picked off one by one like a bunch of… Indians. I
will nobly sacrifice my life in the blinding snow…

*(Spotlight goes on. The lights blackout. **ALEXANDER** is no where near the spotlight. As he heads for the spot, the spotlight goes out, and the other lights come up full. The snow machine drops another discharge out the window.)*

...to save what is left of my home, my family, and...

*(**ALEXANDER** dashes to the spotlight mark. Unfortunately, it doesn't come on, and he makes a fool out of himself.)*

...the snow.

BETTE. How do we know that you aren't the killer? I saw the way you looked at Drools. In that special way.

ALEXANDER. I'll not sit here...

*(Realizing he is standing, **BRENT** sits on the painted-on chair with a frozen smile on his face.)*

...and listen to your lies another moment.

*(**BRENT** rises.)*

Take your hands off me!

*(**BETTE** crosses the stage and puts her hands on **ALEXANDER**.)*

(throwing her hands off)

I must go!

*(**ALEXANDER** goes to make his dramatic exit out the front door and pulls the doorknob off in his hand. The door remains closed. He fumbles with the doorknob, trying to make his exit.)*

I must go!

BETTE. Ha ha!

ALEXANDER. And here I go... I am going...

BETTE. You are going...

ALEXANDER. I am going... Ha ha! I will use the back door!

VICTOR. Phillip! Phillip! Get out here and repair the set!

*(**PHILLIP** enters and tries screwing the doorknob back on.)*

BRENT. Mr. Le Pewe we haven't gone two minutes without you interfering.

PIGGY. What's the problem, Shakespeare?

BRENT. Just once I would like us to rehearse with some continue-itty. At Arena Stage, we never stopped for inferior set design.

PHILLIP. "Inferior?" I like that.

VICTOR. Don't listen to him, Phillip. You did a wonderful job with the budget you were allowed.

PHILLIP. *(to* **BRENT***)*

You try building a set for $35 sometime, Mr. Bigtime Actor.

PIGGY. Maybe you're just too professional for us here, Mr. Regional Theater.

DICK. Hey, come on. I gotta be at the shop at nine in the morning. Fix the damn doorknob and let's finish this thing.

PIGGY. Let's go, Le Pewe. And do something about Sharon Stone over there. You want to turn the audience's stomach with her laying like that? You can see up to China. We're not putting on a geriatric peepshow.

VICTOR. Phillip, get that doorknob on!

(**PHILLIP** *goes back to work on the door.*)

PIGGY. *(to* **MONA***)* And Mona, watch it when you slap her. You want to knock her teeth into the front row? You could blind someone with porcelain.

VICTOR. *(motioning to ignore him)* Listen to him, Mona.

PHILLIP. All fixed, Mr. Le Pewe.

PIGGY. Let's go.

(re: lights)

We're burning up the juice.

VICTOR. Phillip! Go out and buy a small headset for Helen Keller's grandmother. We can pipe her lines in from backstage!

PHILLIP. Brilliant, Mr. Le Pewe!

VICTOR. Places, everyone! We'll take it from… Phillip!

PHILLIP. "Foolish heroic madman! He'll die from the frost before he makes it to the road!" Bette.

BETTE. I know my lines.

(The actors take their places and resume the play.)

Foolish heroic madman! He'll die of frost before he makes it to the road. Yes, my darling brother, it was I who murdered father. But you see, I had to. He wouldn't even share his cheese with me. Gouda cheese. Sliced thin. And mother…you couldn't keep your hands off him. You loved rubbing in the fact that I couldn't get a mate. You had father. Alexander had all those women. Drools had his blowup dolls. But me? What did I have? Nothing. Just a stable full of horses, and a lot of dreams.

*(No one enters. **MONA** repeats the cue-line.)*

Just a stable full of horses, and a lot of dreams.

(Pause.)

That's all I had.

(Pause.)

*(to **VICTOR**)*

And that's all you're getting.

*(Work lights come on, as **VICTOR** charges down the aisle.)*

VICTOR. Where is Chaz Looney?

*(**PHILLIP** enters.)*

PHILLIP. I don't know. I was at the store.

VICTOR. Stage managers don't say "I don't know."

MONA. Chaz, get your ass out here!

*(**MONA** opens the set's front door and we see **CHAZ LOONEY** and **CANDY APPLES** molesting each other. **CHAZ** is in his boxers, his pants down around his*

ankles. They are in the midst of a passionate kiss. They freeze in shock.)

ALL. Ooh.

*(**MONA** slams the door shut. **PIGGY** bolts down the aisle.)*

PIGGY. What the hell was that?

DICK. That was God Awful. That's what that was.

PIGGY. *(Leaping onstage)* Don't move!

*(Everyone moves away from the front door. **PIGGY** opens the door and yanks out **CHAZ** as he desperately tries pulling up his pants.)*

*(strangling **CHAZ**)*

I'll kill you! I'll murder you! I'll beat you until you bleed! And then I'll fire you!

*(**BRENT** and **DICK** restrain **PIGGY** as he lunges at **CHAZ**.)*

CHAZ. Help me. Help me. Save me. Candy!

CANDY. Don't Piggy. We couldn't help it. It was bigger than the both of us.

PHILLIP. It's true! It's true!

*(**PIGGY** throws **CHAZ** off the stage.)*

PIGGY. Get your ass out of my theater. You'll never work again. I'll blackball you. You are finished in this business.

MONA. You think he had a future?

CHAZ. *(standing in the aisle, his pants around his ankles)* Please, Mr. Banks. This is my first New York break. Please don't fire me.

MONA. This is pathetic.

VICTOR. Mr. Banks, we cannot fire Mr. Looney. We open tomorrow night. We will never replace him in time.

ALABAMA. Mr. Banks, my play cannot withstand another change. You've done enough to it. Please, sir. At least allow us to get by the opening night critics.

VICTOR. Oh, God. Give us tomorrow night at least. If we don't get past the critics, we'll lose at the box office. It could mean a flop.

PIGGY. "Flop?"

VICTOR. None of us can afford to fail. I am Victor Le Pewe. I am the director. I have clippings. Phillip, my pills!

*(**PHILLIP** attends to the spasmodic **VICTOR**.)*

DICK. And not for nothing. But my cousin Marty will be out front tomorrow night. He could buy the movie rights if he likes it.

*(**PIGGY** approaches **CHAZ**.)*

PIGGY. Listen, Chaz-hole, I'm a kind-hearted individual. You got tomorrow night. After that you're history.

CHAZ. But I spent weeks rehearsing.

PIGGY. Take it or leave it.

ALL. Take it.

CHAZ. *(sobbing)* I'd just like to say…it's an honor to do one night of your show, Mr. Banks…

*(**CHAZ** exits backstage, crying. **VICTOR** heads down in to the audience.)*

VICTOR. Places, everyone. Drools entrance.

*(Everyone gets into place. **CHAZ** is heard sobbing.)*

ALABAMA. Victor. Banks is killing our show.

PIGGY. Candy, I want to be speaking on you. After rehearsal. I'll be in your dressing room. Waiting.

CANDY. Yes, Daddy.

*(**PIGGY** exits backstage, humiliated. All eyes glare at **CANDY**. She exits backstage in tears.)*

*(to **MONA**, in tears)*

I hate you.

VICTOR. Places!!

CONSTANCE. *(entering)* Is it me?

VICTOR. You're dead!

CONSTANCE. What?

VICTOR. You're dead!

CONSTANCE. Am I? I always thought it would be like this. Where's Laurence? Where are Hume and Jessica? We have so much to catch up on.

*(**CRAWFORD** exits backstage.)*

VICTOR. Go!

*(Stage lights come up. **MONA** gets into character and continues.)*

BETTE. Just a stable full of horses and a lot of dreams.

(Sound effects: Raging Windstorm)

*(**CHAZ LOONEY** enters through the archway, crying full throttle for being fired. He carries a small snub-nosed prop gun and a copy of "Show Business" casting calls. He tries acting through his sobs.)*

DROOLS. *(in tears)* Thank you for that lovely confession, Bette.

VICTOR. Stop crying, dammit.

MONA. What is wrong with you?

CHAZ. I can't help it, Mr. Le Pewe.

CANDY. *(popping her head in through the window)* For me, Chaz.

*(**CHAZ** nods. No tears.)*

VICTOR. Don't you two know when to quit? Miss Apples, offstage! Mr. Looney, straighten up!

CHAZ. *(crying)* I'll try.

*(**CHAZ** motions that he'll need a moment to prepare. He pauses, shakes down, etc. "preparing" for his role. **MONA** shoots **VICTOR** daggers, and sits to wait. **DICK SCORSESE** leans up off the floor and motions to his*

watch. After a beat of preparing, **CHAZ** *straightens up, composed. He motions that the scene may continue.)*

MONA. You're sure?

*(***CHAZ*** is now in character, ready for some serious acting.)*

BETTE. Drools! You're a butler! Not a policeman!

*(***CHAZ*** cries full throttle.)*

DROOLS. Born to serve, Miss Bette. And today I serve the call of justice.

*(***BETTE*** pulls out a large barrel revolver that makes his gun look uselessly puny.)*

BETTE. Drop that gun!

DROOLS. *(throwing away his puny gun)* Very clever, Bette.

BETTE. Ha ha! Foolish ignorant misguided manservant!

*(***BETTE*** shoots **DROOLS**. He staggers all over the stage, dying.)*

DROOLS. Ah, what a sad day for the Barringtons…ah…

*(***DROOLS*** dies stage left and proceeds to sob to himself for being fired. **CANDY** enters, out of character, crying.)*

PENELOPE. Oh, I couldn't sleep. I thought I heard a noise.

BETTE. Really?

PENELOPE. What's happened to Drools?

BETTE. Hunting accident.

PENELOPE. *(back in character)* Funny. With that expression on his face, he looks like… By Jove, I thought he looked familiar.

BETTE. What are you babbling about?

PENELOPE. *(caressing his body)* It's my brother Whiff. My little brother Whiff who was stolen in infancy by a band of wandering gypsies. I have searched high and low for him all these many years.

BETTE. Well, now you've found him. And I hope that the two of you will be very happy together.

(As **BETTE** *points her gun,* **ALEXANDER** *enters the front door.)*

(Sound effects: Raging Windstorm)

*(***PHILLIP*** *can be seen throwing handfuls of snow in after him.)*

ALEXANDER. Drop that gun, you conniving bitch!

BETTE. *(turning her back on* **PENELOPE***)* Never!

*(***BETTE*** *points and shoots her gun at* **ALEXANDER***'s shoulder, as* **PENELOPE** *grabs a breakaway bottle from inside the bar.)*

PENELOPE. Look out, Alexander, look out!

*(***CANDY*** *stands blocking* **MONA** *from the audience and smashes the bottle on her head.)*

MONA. Wait a minute! Wait a minute!

BRENT. What now?

CANDY. What did I do?

MONA. Learn your blocking. It's my death scene for Christ's sake.

(to **VICTOR,** *out front)*

She's standing right in front of me. They're paying to see Mona Monet. I think they should get to see my face when I die.

BRENT. Oh, Mona. Don't worry. They'll be watching you die all night long.

MONA. Up yours, Pen-la-pee-pee.

BRENT. Mr. Le Pewe! Could we go on, please? Am I the only professional in this company?

*(***CANDY*** *grabs a second bottle and crosses between* **MONA** *and* **BRENT***.)*

CANDY. *(re: A Second Breakaway Bottle)* What are these made out of anyway? Candy?

MONA. Sugar.

CANDY. Sugar Candy. Like me.

BRENT. Could we go on, please!

CANDY. Okay!

(*back in character as* **PENELOPE**)

Look out, Alexander. Look out!

(**CANDY** *swings the bottle over her head, breaking the nose of* **BRENT** *who stands behind her. In a continuous swing, she cracks* **MONA** – *who stands in front of her* – *in the head and knocks her out.* **MONA** *falls unconscious to the floor. In levels. The bottle never breaks. And* **CANDY** *keeps hitting her with it.*)

CANDY. It won't break.

BRENT. She broke my nose!

VICTOR. (*from out front*) Going on.

BRENT. She broke my nose!

VICTOR. (*from out front*) Going on, please, Mr. Professional.

PENELOPE. Oh, Alexander. Your shoulder. Does it hurt much?

ALEXANDER. (*in agony, blood pouring from his nose*) No. It's just a flesh wound. But Bette is dead. And so are mother. Father. Inspector Mounds.

(**DICK SCORSESE** *sneezes.*)

And the telephone.

PENELOPE. And Whiff. My little brother Whiff.

(*Sound effects: Dramatic Music Builds To Crescendo*)

ALEXANDER. The brother who was stolen in infancy by a band of wandering gypsies you were telling me about on the ride over here?

PENELOPE. Yes. And now my search has ended.

ALEXANDER. And we can go on with our lives.

PENELOPE. Oh, Alexander. Hold me. Hold me. Don't touch me.

(*Spotlight on.* **ALEXANDER** *steps forward, every step painful.*)

ALEXANDER. The snow is melting. At last.

(**ALEXANDER** *and* **PENELOPE** *pose dramatically as the music builds. As they pose,* **VICTOR** *walks up to the stage with a handful of notes.*)

VICTOR. And curtain. Worklights, please!

(*Sound effects: The Music Abruptly Stops.*)

(*Worklights on.*)

BRENT. My nose! She broke my nose!

VICTOR. Phillip! Revive Miss Monet. May I have the entire company assembled for some notes, please?

(**PHILLIP** *revives* **MONA**. **CHAZ** *gets* **CRAWFORD**, *as the actors gather to hear notes.*)

DICK. Is this going to take long? I have to get up pretty damn early.

VICTOR. Mr. Miller? Would you care to address the company?

(*All eyes focus on* **ALABAMA MILLER**, *now completely drunk. They wait for words of praise.*)

ALABAMA. My life...is over. It's meaningless. What's the point? You know?

(**ALABAMA** *breaks down in a mixture of tears and scotch.* **VICTOR** *turns back to the cast.*)

VICTOR. Thank you, Mr. Miller. Kids, we have a super show here. It's pure Le Pewe.

BRENT. (*re:* **CRAWFORD**) What do you plan on doing about...?

VICTOR. Phillip!

(**PHILLIP** *takes out two headsets. One tiny, clear and unobtrusive, and one big and bulky – like an air traffic controller would wear. He hands the small one to* **CRAWFORD**.

PHILLIP. Miss Crawford, try this on. We can conceal the receiver under your wig and no one will be the wiser.

CONSTANCE. Try catching one when it's raining.

(No one has any idea what she's talking about.)

DICK. Can't we just use a bullhorn?

VICTOR. Let's try it once. People, places, please. Miss Crawford's first entrance.

(EVERYONE moves into position. PHILLIP opens the front door to exit backstage and PIGGY staggers in. Stabbed through the chest with scissors. He gasps for air. Speechless. Dying. AD LIB COMMOTION.)

VICTOR. Omigod.

(PIGGY falls forward. Dead. EVERYONE gathers around. ALABAMA takes his pulse.)

CANDY. Piggy!

(PHILLIP runs backstage to find the killer.)

VICTOR. Phillip! Don't go back there!

(ALABAMA stands back.)

ALABAMA. He's dead.

MONA. What? Oh, God.

(PHILLIP enters.)

PHILLIP. There's no one back there!

VICTOR. But there has to be.

PHILLIP. There's no one I tell you!

ALABAMA. That means...one of us...

MONA. Omigod. He's dead.

CANDY. You mean...

CRAWFORD. Murderrrr!

(Sound effects: Ominous Music Sting)

(Everyone looks at CRAWFORD. EVERYONE looks out front.)

(Blackout)

End of Act One

ACT TWO

(Intermission)

(Prior to the start of Act Two, **PHILLIP** *re-sets the stage, sweeps, goes through the crowds passing out programs, blinks the lights, cleans the lobby, checks ticket stubs, etc. He is dressed in his same stage manager blacks, with the addition of an opening night carnation.)*

(Intro music: The same ominous harpsichord music. Lights up on the Barrington Estate. The setting is the same as before, except **DROOLS** *now sports a blue French beret, pencil mustache, and a cigarette with his butler uniform.)*

DROOLS. Ah, what a sad day for zee Barringtons. Especially Lord Barrington, who was found horribly murdered as he ate cheese in the library. Brie cheese. Sliced thin. I am Drools, zee French butler. I have slaved for zis family since I was a little boy, as my father did before me and his father before him, and my grandmother beside him, and my mother beneath her.

(The door chimes.)

Ah, zee door is chiming. I must answer it, as I have done since... Hey. Why don't I just answer zee door?

*(***DROOLS** *stubs out his cigarette and crosses to the front door, in French. He opens the door.)*

(Sound effects: Raging Windstorm)

(In walks **ALEXANDER BARRINGTON** *— wearing a big tongue depressor as a splint surgically taped to his nose. and his new bride* **PENELOPE** *— minus the suitcase this time. Enthusiastic bursts of snow are thrown in*

after them. **ALEXANDER** *and* **PENELOPE** *pose together D.S.C.)*

Young Alexander Barrington.

ALEXANDER. Drools. Kindly Drools. Ever faithful. Ever true.

DROOLS. And who is the young "mademoiselle" I see before me?

ALEXANDER. Drools, I'd like you to meet my new bride... Phyllis.

PENELOPE. A delight.

DROOLS. The delight is mine. As well as young Alexander's I've no doubt in my French mind.

ALEXANDER. *(Slipping into a french accent)*

Ah, Drools. It's a zad day for zee Barringtons.

DROOLS. May I take your coats?

(**DROOLS** *takes their coats and hat and hangs them on the coat rack. This time, they surprisingly stay up.* **PHILLIP** *pokes his head out and gives* **CHAZ** *an "okay" sign.)*

ALEXANDER. Is mother about?

DROOLS. She's been under quite a strain. Finding the lord like that. Face down in the Brie. Sliced thin.

ALEXANDER. *(posing dramatically)* Poor Mother.

PENELOPE. *(posed identically)* Poor thing.

ALEXANDER. How is she?

DROOLS. Hasn't touched a dairy product since. Not even Le Yogurt.

ALEXANDER. And my sister...

(disgusted)

Bette...

(back to normal)

Has she arrived yet?

DROOLS. Yes, she's come, sir. Arrive-ed-a zis morning. Singing "Alouetta, jante alouetta."

PENELOPE. How odd.

ALEXANDER. Not as odd as having a French butler.

DROOLS. Ah, life is strange. I'll see if the Lady Barrington is up and around. May I take your zuitcase?

*(**PENELOPE** has none. But mimes one, egg on face. **DROOLS** mimes taking it from her. And it's heavy. He drags it offstage.)*

Please help yourself to the sherry. It will warm you from zee winter chill.

*(**DROOLS** exits through the archway.)*

PENELOPE. There's a chill in the air. A chill about this house, Alexander. An evil chill. That I cannot explain. I am frightened. Hold me. Hold me.

*(**PENELOPE** and **ALEXANDER** embrace.)*

ALEXANDER. You're all right. As long as I'm around, Penny-loafer.

PENELOPE. I feel better knowing that you are near.

ALEXANDER. I'll never leave you. Never.

*(**ALEXANDER** steps forward into a spotlight as the stage lights blackout. In the spill of the spotlight, we see **ALABAMA MILLER** sneak on, wearing a choir robe, carrying a music stand. He sets it up DSL and exits backstage. **BRENT** and **CANDY** don't see him.)*

The snow. Falling snow. White snow. Snow everywhere. Snow. Each flake different and unique in a melan"ch"oly way. Yet together…a mass…of constant white…

*(Spotlight off – stage lights up full as **ALEXANDER** steps back into the scene. Snow falls outside the window – from a cheaply made "snow machine" hanging above the window.)*

PENELOPE. What are you trying to tell me, Alexander?

*(**ALEXANDER** crosses to the fireplace.)*

ALEXANDER. I was born and raised in this house, Pippy… Pippy… Pippy. I lived here my entire life.

(**ALABAMA** *runs past the window carrying a 576 page manuscript, chased by* **PHILLIP**.)

With the exception of school and college and day camp. And the week I was kidnapped by the man in the Blue Mask. This home is my blood. This home and...

(*Spotlight on – stage lights out as* **ALEXANDER** *steps forward. In the spill of the spotlight,* **ALABAMA** *dashes on, determined to save his play.* **PHILLIP** *tries grabbing him from backstage, but* **ALABAMA** *breaks away and sets up his manuscript downstage left on the music stand.*)

... The Snow...

(*Spotlight off – stage lights up as* **ALEXANDER** *steps back into the scene.*)

(*posing at fireplace*)

There's nothing I wouldn't do to keep it. Nothing.

(**INSPECTOR MOUNDS** *enters from the archway.*)

INSPECTOR. "Anything?" What do you mean by "anything?"

ALABAMA. "Nothing." He means "Nothing."

(**ALEXANDER, PENELOPE** , *and* **DICK** *freeze. They decide to plow ahead.*)

PENELOPE. Oh!

ALEXANDER. (*to* **INSPECTOR**) Who the hell are you?

(*to* **ALABAMA**)

And who the hell are you?

INSPECTOR. Me?

ALEXANDER. Yes. No. I mean, yes.

INSPECTOR. Inspector Mounds.

ALABAMA. And I am the ghost of Lord Barrington. Here to make sure everything is said correctly. I am the ever-present specter of death that looms over us all.

ALEXANDER. Beg your pardon?

(**INSPECTOR MOUNDS** *dramatically poses at the fireplace – with his foot set on the log.*)

INSPECTOR. Inspector Mounds. Scotland Yard. I'm investigating your late father's death.

(eying **ALABAMA***)*

Musical sort of fellow, was he?

ALEXANDER. And what have you found? We have nothing to hide here.

INSPECTOR. Nothing?

ALABAMA. "Nothing." Everything comes from nothing. All of time comes from a single point. A man who has nothing has everything. A man who has it all has less. A man with less than nothing is everything I give my all.

ALEXANDER. Nothing that can't be explained.

INSPECTOR. Explained?

ALEXANDER. And what else do you know, Inspector?

INSPECTOR. We know that your late father didn't die accidentally.

ALEXANDER. You mean…

*(***DICK*** *waits to see if* **ALABAMA** *will interrupt him, but* **ALABAMA** *motions "No, go ahead.")*

INSPECTOR. Murderrr!

(Sound effects: Ominous Music Sting)

PENELOPE. Oh, Alexander. Hold me. Touch me. Thrill me.

(Spotlight on – stage lights out, as **ALEXANDER** *steps forward.)*

ALEXANDER. Looks like snow.

(Spotlight off – stage lights up, as **ALEXANDER** *steps back into the scene.)*

INSPECTOR. Would you mind answering some questions, Mr. Barrington?

ALEXANDER. I have nothing to hide.

ALABAMA. What has a man to hide, if he hides himself?

INSPECTOR. The reading of the will will tale the tell. Tell the tale, I mean.

ALEXANDER. *(motioning to* **ALABAMA***)* Meaning?

ALABAMA. Another link in the evolutionary chain.

INSPECTOR. Exactly what was your sister Bette's relationship with your late father?

(**MONA MONET** *sweeps in as* **BETTE.***)*

(Sound effects: The Audience Goes Wild.)

(**BETTE** *bows and blows kisses.* **BRENT** *burns.)*

BETTE. Marvelous, Inspector. We got along divinely. I was like a daughter to him and he was like a father to me. I miss him so.

(flicking away a tear)

It's hard to believe he's really gone.

ALEXANDER. He's still with us, in a way.

(**DROOLS** *pops in to deliver a punch line.)*

DROOLS. Filet mignon! He's not really gone. He's still in the study. They haven't come for the body yet. Snow and all.

(**DROOLS** *sees* **ALABAMA** *and exits with a questioned look.)*

BETTE. Hello, brother.

ALEXANDER. *(spitting on* **ALABAMA** *on purpose)* Hello… Bette!

BETTE. Who is that?

ALABAMA. I am the ghost of your father. The ever-present specter of death that looms over us all.

BETTE. Oh.

(to **PENELOPE***)*

You must be the new one.

ALEXANDER. Bette…this is… Po-po.

PENELOPE. Delighted. What did you mean, "New one?"

ALABAMA. A rebirth. Everyone is replaceable. Like parts of an engine.

INSPECTOR. Yes. What did you mean? I didn't quite follow that myself.

BETTE. Didn't dear brother tell you? You're number thirteen. Unlucky number thirteen! Ha ha!

PENELOPE. Thirteen? Thirteen what?

BETTE. Why, thirteen wives, you little unsuspecting fool!

PENELOPE. I thought I was the first.

BETTE. Naive foolish petulant child!

ALEXANDER. You are the first, Penicillin. The first that meant anything.

PENELOPE. Alexander...what happened to them? Were they pretty?

ALEXANDER. They were all lovely. Especially Gwendolyn. With her fair skin, tight sweaters, and massively large jugs.

ALABAMA. Strike that!

PENELOPE. Where are they now?

ALEXANDER. She was buried with them.

PENELOPE. You mean…

ALEXANDER. Dead.

PENELOPE. You mean?

BETTE. Murderrr!

(Sound effects: Ominous Music Sting)

ALEXANDER. I always meant to tell you that, dear.

ALABAMA. A taking of a life.

*(**PHILLIP** enters from backstage, wearing a choir robe, carrying a thick roll of masking tape. As **ALABAMA** rambles on, **PHILLIP** methodically unrolls and cuts off two pieces of tape which he uses to tape **ALABAMA**'s hands behind his back. **PHILLIP** take the scarf from around his neck and gags **ALABAMA** with it, mid-sentence.)*

ALABAMA.... So simple. So free. And yet so binding. And confusing. How can one judge a murderer unless he himself has murdered or been murdered? Whose values of good and evil are the norm? What if our sense of values is based on the wrong standards? How do we balance the scales? I think this is the one lesson my son and daughter have learned in this moment. If only they could cut the ties that bind them...

(gagged)

Mmm!

(PHILLIP *exits backstage, making a sly "OK" sign to the others.)*

INSPECTOR. Interesting, Mr. Barrington. If you'll excuse me.

(The **INSPECTOR** *goes to exit into the painted on doorway. He catches himself and exits through the archway.)*

BETTE. Ha ha!

(ALABAMA *tries to remove his tape during the following:)*

Juries can be bought. You never did explain that blood on your socks.

(DROOLS *enters.)*

DROOLS. Escargot! Monsieur Barrington, your mother can't wait to zee you. I told her that you had arrive-ed-a and her face lit up like...the face of a gentleman at the Follies Bergere. Presenting Lady Barrington!

(The actors cross their fingers. Right on cue, **LADY BARRINGTON** *enters. She wears the wrong headset. She wears the bulky Air Traffic Controller looking headset.)*

PHILLIP. *(off)* Okay, Miss Crawford. Walk over to the sofa and turn around.

(LADY BARRINGTON *walks to the sofa and turns around.)*

ALEXANDER. Mother! It's been so long!

PHILLIP. *(off)* Say "Alexander, my boy. You've come home."

LADY BARRINGTON. Alexander, my boy. You've come home.

PHILLIP. *(off)* "I don't know how to tell you this, son."

LADY BARRINGTON. I don't know how to tell you this, son.

PHILLIP. "But Daddy is dead."

LADY BARRINGTON. But Daddy is dead.

PHILLIP. *(off)* "He died eating cheese."

LADY BARRINGTON. He died eating cheese.

PHILLIP. *(off)* "Gouda cheese. Sliced thin."

LADY BARRINGTON. Gouda cheese. Sliced thin.

ALEXANDER. I know, Mother. That's why I've come.

PHILLIP. *(off)* "What is this?"

LADY BARRINGTON. What is this?

PHILLIP. *(off)* Cross him.

> (**CRAWFORD** *blesses* **ALEXANDER** *with the Sign-of-the-Cross.*)

PHILLIP. *(off)* Go to Penelope!

LADY BARRINGTON. Go to Penelope.

ALEXANDER. What?

PHILLIP. *(off)* Do it, dammit.

LADY BARRINGTON. Do it, dammit!

ALEXANDER. *(Jumping to* **PENELOPE**'s *side)*
Very well, Mother. This is my new bride, Pennsylvania.

PHILLIP. *(off)* "Such a pretty child. So young. So sad."

LADY BARRINGTON. Such a pretty child. So young. So sad.

PHILLIP. "How old are you?"

LADY BARRINGTON. That's none of your Goddamn business.

ALEXANDER. Huh? What is?

PENELOPE. Twenty-three and one half.

ALEXANDER. What?

PHILLIP. *(off)* "Pity."

LADY BARRINGTON. Pity.

BETTE. If you knew what was good for you, you'd take the first train out of here.

PHILLIP. Hold on a minute.

LADY BARRINGTON. Hold on a minute.

ALEXANDER. What?

*(Sound effects: A song from **PHILLIP**'s Ipod)*

PHILLIP. *(off)* Son of a bitch.

LADY BARRINGTON. Son of a bitch.

PHILLIP. *(off)* No!

LADY BARRINGTON. No!

ALEXANDER. Huh?

DROOLS. Zee trains are not running because of zee snow. We are all trapped here like Napoleon at Waterloo.

ALABAMA. Mmm!

PHILLIP. *(off)* Say, "There is no escape from her fate. Your fate is sealed, my dear."

LADY BARRINGTON. There is no escape from her fate. Your fate is sealed, my dear.

PHILLIP. *(off)* Point to the window.

LADY BARRINGTON. Point to the window.

PHILLIP. Point to the window!

LADY BARRINGTON. Point to the window!!

*(Everyone points to the window, reluctantly. The cardboard snow climbs up. **ALEXANDER** steps forward, but there is no spotlight.)*

ALEXANDER. Especially in this snow…

*(He steps back into the scene and the spotlight goes on. **ALEXANDER** steps back into the spotlight, saying nothing. He just stands there like a fool. Stage lights come up, and he steps back into the scene. **INSPECTOR MOUNDS** enters.)*

BETTE. Inspector Mounds. You're still here.

INSPECTOR. And so are we all. I'm glad I have you all here. I have found conclusive evidence which will point conclusively to the killer of Lord Barrington.

(All gasp – including **PHILLIP** *over the headset.* **CRAWFORD** *gasps two beats late.)*

Please be seated.

(All sit, as **PHILLIP** *yells at* **CRAWFORD** *over the headset:)*

PHILLIP. *(off)* Sit down!

LADY BARRINGTON. *(to* **BRENT***)* Sit down!

*(***BRENT** *rises and sits again.)*

PHILLIP. *(off)* You're ruining everything!

LADY BARRINGTON. *(to* **BRENT***)*
You're ruining everything!

PHILLIP. *(off)* We're going to fire you!

LADY BARRINGTON. We're going to fire you!

ALEXANDER. What?

PHILLIP. *(off)* Get off!

LADY BARRINGTON. Get off!

PHILLIP. *(off)* Shut up!

LADY BARRINGTON. Shut up!

BETTE. Go on, Inspector.

PHILLIP. *(off)* Miss Crawford, walk to the archway. We're going to replace you!

*(***CRAWFORD** *walks to the archway and addresses* **DROOLS***.)*

CONSTANCE. We're going to replace you!

CHAZ. Replace who?

*(***CRAWFORD** *is yanked offstage.)*

BETTE. Go on, Inspector!

*(***VICTOR LE PEWE** *enters, dressed in an identical* **LADY BARRINGTON** *costume. He is petrified.)*

VICTOR. *(As* **LADY BARRINGTON***)*

Yes… Go on, Inspector.

(ad libbing)

I haven't been myself lately.

*(***VICTOR*** *sits on loveseat.)*

INSPECTOR. Uh…yes. The murderer is someone in this room!

(All gasp. **CRAWFORD** *gasps backstage, two beats later.)*

I found these two items on the body of the lord. Buried in the Gouda. Sliced thin. This letter.

(All gasp. **ALABAMA** *breaks his hands free.)*

And this brassiere!

*(***INSPECTOR*** *holds up bra. All "OOH."* **ALABAMA** *takes out his gag. He is raving mad.)*

ALABAMA. I'm free!

(sees audience)

As we all will be someday. The ever-present specter of death that looms over us all cannot be stifled by the binds of life!

INSPECTOR. *(going faster and faster now)* The contents of this letter, written in the murderer's own hand…

ALABAMA. The handwriting is on the wall. Our society has been forewarned!

INSPECTOR. Together with this brassiere…

ALABAMA. The mark of human sexuality. Carried with us through life much like a perfectly proportioned hand-carved mahogany credenza. Quietly, yet authoritatively dominating its surroundings. We are the faithful custodians of life's wood works. And yet, so often we neglect to polish our credenzas. Are there none so deaf as those who will not hear? Are there none so short as those who will not grow? I think that this is the conclusion the Inspector has come to, in this his final hour.

INSPECTOR. Right. And now I can conclusively conclude that the murderer is none other than...

(Quick blackout. There is an immediate round of loud gunfire.)

CHAZ. What the hell was that?

*(Silence, followed by scuffling in the dark. The lights come up full and all the actors are caught offguard, looking around for the location of the gunfire. **PENELOPE** is once again in her corset. **INSPECTOR MOUNDS** places his plastic dagger under his arm and dies. **ALEXANDER** goes to take his pulse. The **INSPECTOR**'s arm shoots up early, and **ALEXANDER** takes his pulse.)*

ALEXANDER. Good God! He's dead!

*(**CANDY** lets out a blood-curdling scream as **ALABAMA** staggers forward. He is riddled with bullets and covered with blood. He clutches his chest. The other actors jump back in real fear.)*

ALABAMA. I've been shot...

*(**ALABAMA** staggers and falls dead. The "actors" break character and react with horror.)*

CHAZ. That's not supposed to happen!

*(**MONA** nudges him to shut up. **BRENT** takes **ALABAMA**'s pulse.)*

BRENT. Good God. He's dead...

(sees audience and gets back into character)

...too.

*(**DICK** peeks out from his "dead" position.)*

CANDY. You mean...

VICTOR. *(as **LADY BARRINGTON**)* Murder?

BRENT. Two murders.

(Sound effects: Ominous Music Sting)

CHAZ. You bet your ass it's murder! We should have called the police when Banks got killed! I told you! I told you!

(**CANDY** *runs to* **CHAZ** *for protection. They are scared out of their wits.* **BRENT**, **MONA** *and* **VICTOR** *decide to go on with the show.*)

ALEXANDER. I know it's hard to accept…father's ghost's death…but…we must go on. The eyes of the world are upon us…now..in our hour of grief.

CHAZ. What?

ALEXANDER. *(pointedly)* I said…the "eyes" of the world are upon us. We-must-go-on!

(**EVERYONE** *turns and sees the audience staring back at them. The show must go on.*)

BETTE. How right you are. Ha ha. Some might even be casting a critical eye upon us.

(**DICK** *peeks out to his cousin* **MARTIN SCORSESE** *sitting in the audience and waves.*)

DICK. Marty! Marty!

(**DICK** *mimes stabbing himself under the arm with the rubber knife.*)

BETTE. Need we review this any further?

ALEXANDER. Where were we?

(**ALEXANDER** *pulls* **PENELOPE** *to him, and away from the butler.*)

BETTE. Well, we know it's not Inspector Mounds.

(*as* **MONA**)

Or do we?

(**DICK** *shakes his head "no."*)

CHAZ. Well, we know it's not… Lord Barrington.

ALEXANDER. That's true. There he is. The ever-present specter of death that looms over us all.

VICTOR. *(As* **LADY BARRINGTON**)

Then…it must be someone in this room…

(*All exchange looks of suspicion.* **CRAWFORD** *wanders past the window, out in the snow, wearing her headset and not knowing where she is.*)

PENELOPE. I feel faint.

CHAZ. Me too.

ALEXANDER. You should lie down, Penis-lips. I'll take you off to rest. Where shall we go to rest, Drools?

CHAZ. Can I come, too?

ALEXANDER. No.

DROOLS. Anyplace but zee study. It's...

(seeing ALABAMA's body)

...occupied?

ALEXANDER. Mother, will you be all right?

BETTE. With you gone, at least she'll be alive!

ALEXANDER. Why you dirty bitch!

(ALEXANDER goes to slap BETTE theatrically but can't due to her cigarette holder. Instead, he blows on her.)

BETTE. The truth always...blows.

ALEXANDER. I'll be back, Mother. Stay alive until I do.

VICTOR. I will, son, I will.

(CHAZ points to ALABAMA's lifeless body.)

CHAZ. Hey. Why don't you take that with you when you go?

ALEXANDER. Very well, Drools.

(ALEXANDER forces a disgusted CANDY to take the hands and feet of the corpse and drag ALABAMA out the front door.)

Would you get the door, Mother?

(VICTOR opens the front door, as ALEXANDER and PENELOPE exit with ALABAMA's body. VICTOR closes the door, a twitching wreck. ALEXANDER and PENELOPE re-enter. ALEXANDER makes wind sounds and "acts" cold from the great outdoors. They exit through the archway. DROOLS crosses to the spasmodic VICTOR and shakes him violently.)

DROOLS. You must be shaken. You must be shaken.

BETTE. A drink for Lady Barrington, Drools.

CHAZ. I'm not going out there.

VICTOR. *(as* **LADY BARRINGTON***)* I sure would like a hot toddy, Drools!

BETTE. He lives to serve you, Mother.

CHAZ. Right now, I'm more interested in the living than the serving.

BETTE. *(ad libbing)* I shall go get your drink, Mother.

(**BETTE** *takes* **DROOLS***' tray, and exits through the archway.*)

VICTOR. *(As* **LADY BARRINGTON***)*

I guess this leaves us quite alone... Drools...

(**CRAWFORD** *wanders on stage, still wearing her headset.*)

CHAZ. Not quite.

VICTOR. *(as* **LADY BARRINGTON***, oblivious)* And we'll never know what Inspector Mounds was going to tell us.

CONSTANCE. Why do you say that, Bette?

(**VICTOR** *turns and sees* **CRAWFORD***.)*

DROOLS. Ah, it's Lady Barrington!

(turning to **VICTOR** *and passing the buck)*

Then...who are you?

VICTOR. I...uh...I...uh... I'm Lady Barrington's sister.

DROOLS. From Italy.

VICTOR. From Italy.

DROOLS. Which would explain that mustache on your face.

VICTOR. I am Lady Barrington's sister from Italy.

DROOLS. And I am Drools, zee French butler.

(**VICTOR** *goes insane when he hears the word "French" and strangles* **CHAZ** *until* **CRAWFORD** *begins speaking again.*)

CONSTANCE. Why do you say that, Bette?

PHILLIP. *(off)* I lost my place!

CONSTANCE. I lost my place!

PHILLIP. *(off)* How did you get backstage?

LADY BARRINGTON. How did you get backstage?

CHAZ. What?

PHILLIP. *(off)* What are you doing with that rope?

LADY BARRINGTON. What are you doing with that rope?

PHILLIP. *(off)* Help me, Victor. Ah!

LADY BARRINGTON. Help me, Victor! Ahh!

PHILLIP. *(off)* I'm choking! Urgh!

(**CRAWFORD** *begins choking herself all over the stage.*)

LADY BARRINGTON. I'm choking! Urgh!!

PHILLIP. *(off)* Help me! Help me! Argh!

LADY BARRINGTON. Help me! Help me! Argh!

PHILLIP. *(off)* No! No! Argh! Arghhh…

LADY BARRINGTON. No! No! Argh! Arghhh…

(**LADY BARRINGTON** *dramatically "dies" on the love seat.* **VICTOR** *and* **CHAZ** *stand staring, mouths open.* **VICTOR** *comes to his senses and dashes offstage.*)

VICTOR. Phillip! Phillip!

(**VICTOR** *exits past an entering* **BETTE** *who carries* **LADY BARRINGTON**'s *goblet.* **CHAZ** *is frozen with fear, convinced* **MONA** *is the murderer.*)

CHAZ. Who killed him? Who's back there?

BETTE. The drinks, mum. Shaken by hand. Go off, Drools.

CHAZ. *(hiding behind* **CRAWFORD**) I don't want to. I'm not going anywhere.

BETTE. You think everyone's your servant, don't you, Mother? You pompous, money-hungry, society bitch!

(**BETTE** *slaps* **CRAWFORD**, *smacking her hand on the bulky headset.*)

Ow!

CONSTANCE. Didn't get that one. Come in. Mayday. Mayday.

(**BETTE** *goes to the bar for the goblet.*)

BETTE. Here's your drink.

> (**ALEXANDER** *enters from the archway with the white bedsheet.* **CANDY** *enters with him, hiding behind the sheet, afraid of being backstage. She runs to* **CHAZ** *for protection.*)

CANDY. *(sotto)* Help me. Phillip's dead.

ALEXANDER. I've brought a sheet for Inspector Mounds. It's off your bed…

> *(accidentally spitting in* **CRAWFORD**'s *eye)*

Bette!

BETTE. White. How appropriate.

LADY BARRINGTON. Cheers!

> (**CRAWFORD** *drinks from the goblet and is poisoned to death for real. She chokes and dies on the sofa, desperately trying to signal for help as she coughs, spits, and chokes.* **BRENT** *and* **MONA** *think she is acting.*)

CONSTANCE. *(dropping goblet)* Argh…

MONA. What?

CONSTANCE. *(clutching at her throat)* Argh…

ALEXANDER. What are you trying to say, Mother?

CONSTANCE. Argh…

BETTE. She said, "It tastes delicious."

CONSTANCE. Argh…

ALEXANDER. It sounded like "poison."

> (**CRAWFORD** *gasps one last time, and dies on the sofa. Alexander takes her pulse.*)

My God. She's dead!

> *(realizing)*

She is dead!

DICK. That tears it.

> (**DICK** *crawls offstage underneath his sheet.* **MONA** *and* **BRENT** *exchange looks of fear.* **CHAZ** *flips out.*)

CHAZ. *(to* **MONA***)* You gave her the drink! You gave her the drink! You killed Phillip and you killed her too!

BETTE. Nonsense. She's just sleeping.

CHAZ. That's all, brother. Good night, everyone. It's been fun. Let's go, Candy.

(**CHAZ** *and* **CANDY** *try to exit the stage.* **BRENT** *and* **MONA** *block all the exits.* **BRENT** *and* **MONA***'s show "must go on!")*

ALEXANDER. I must go.

CHAZ & CANDY. We'll go with you.)

ALEXANDER. No you won't.

(*The front door breaks again,* **ALEXANDER** *takes the doorknob in hand and dashes off through the archway.* **CANDY** *slips offstage behind him, but* **CHAZ** *is trapped on stage by* **BETTE***. Throughout* **BETTE***'s big speech,* **CHAZ** *tries desperately to get offstage through the permanently shut front door.)*

BETTE. Foolish heroic madman! He'll die from frost before he makes it to the road. Yes, my darling brother. It was I who murdered father…

CHAZ. *(in tears, trying to pry the front door off its hinges)*
I knew it was you… I told them… I guessed it…

MONA. *(to* **CHAZ***)* No!

(to AUDIENCE, as **BETTE***)*

I mean… Yes. But you see, I had to. He wouldn't share his cheese with me. Gouda cheese. Sliced thin. And Mother…

CHAZ. I knew it… I told them…

MONA. *(to* **CHAZ***)* No!

(as **BETTE***)*

I mean… YES. You loved rubbing in the fact that I couldn't get a mate. You had father. Alexander had all those women. Drools had his blowup dolls. But me? What did I have? Nothing. Just a stable full of horses and a lot of screams. Dreams.

CHAZ. Thank you for that lovely confession, Mona.

(points finger like a gun)

I mean... Bette.

BETTE. Drools! You're a butler! Not a policeman!

CHAZ. I don't care. Drop that gun.

MONA. *(having no gun)* What?

CHAZ. Drop your gun... Please don't kill me...

BETTE. Foolish ignorant misguided manservant!

CHAZ. Ahh!

(**BETTE** *gets her gun and points it at* **CHAZ**. *He runs all over the stage, dodging its aim.* **BETTE** *blocks the archway, so he can't escape.* **CHAZ** *uses* **ALABAMA**'s *music stand as a shield as he dashes all over the set.*)

MONA. Stand still!

CHAZ. No!

BETTE. Foolish ignorant misguided manservant! Ha ha!

CHAZ. Save me. Help me...

(**CHAZ** *is cornered by the fireplace.*)

BETTE. I've got you now.

CHAZ. Please. Oh, please.

(**BETTE** *goes to point her gun at a cowering* **CHAZ**. *He faints before the trigger is ever pulled.* **PENELOPE** *is pushed on through the archway, by* **BRENT**.)

PENELOPE. I couldn't sleep I thought I heard a noise.

(From backstage, we hear horrible noises. Crashing and yelling.)

What's happened to Drools? Chaz! What did you do to him?

BETTE. Nothing yet...

(**DICK SCORSESE**, *still in his* **INSPECTOR** *costume and sheet, barges on stage through the archway. He carries a police revolver.*)

DICK. Nobody leave the stage! He's alive! He's alive!

MONA. What?

(**MONA** *tries to work the "dead* **INSPECTOR***" back into the show.*)

MONA. Inspector Mounds… I thought you were dead!

(**DICK** *sees the audience and realizes he is on stage.*)

DICK. Huh? Oh.

(*as* **INSPECTOR**)

Uh…simply a clever ruse. One of those clever ruses. I have discovered the real murderer. It's…your other little brother… Phillip.

MONA & CANDY. Who?

INSPECTOR. Your other little brother, Phillip.

PENELOPE. Who was also stolen in infancy by a band of wandering gypsies?

INSPECTOR. Exactly.

(**DICK** *rushes offstage with his gun drawn.* **MONA** *and* **CANDY** *stare at each other, completely lost.*)

MONA. Uh…

PENELOPE. I have also searched high and low for Whiff's little brother Phillip all these many years. Too.

BETTE. Uh…well. Now, you've found him. And I hope the three of you will be very happy together.

(**BETTE** *points her gun at* **PENELOPE**. *Suddenly,* **DICK SCORSESE** *races by the window, backstage, followed by* **VICTOR LE PEWE** *– still in* **LADY BARRINGTON**'*s costume, and* **BRENT** *– who pops his head in the window, right on cue.*)

ALEXANDER. Drop that gun, you conniving bitch!

(**BRENT** *follows the others offstage right.*)

BETTE. Never!

PENELOPE. Look out, Alexander. Look out!

(**PHILLIP** *– very much alive – dashes through the archway, carrying a revolver. He puts a finger up*

to his lips, as **CANDY** *and* **MONA** *gasp and freeze.*
DICK, **VICTOR** *and* **BRENT** *run by the window again.*
After they pass, **PHILLIP** *runs offstage in the opposite*
direction.)

MONA. *(pointing at* **PHILLIP***)* Phillip! Your other little
brother Phillip!

PENELOPE. The other brother Phillip who was also stolen
in infancy by a band of wandering gypsies I was telling
you about? And that's all I know.

MONA. Yes! And he's the murderer, you moron!

*(***DICK***,* **VICTOR** *and* **BRENT** *burst through the front*
door like TV cops. After a second of frantic searching,
they realize they are on stage. They freeze as they spot the
audience. They try to exit nonchalantly. Upon hitting
the archway, they all bolt out. They run past the window
in hot pursuit. **PHILLIP** *then enters once again, gun*
drawn – finger up to his lips. The men pass. **PHILLIP**
races out the opposite direction.)

I don't know what to say.

DICK, **VICTOR** *and* **BRENT** *enter through the archway.*
PHILLIP *enters through the front door.* **PHILLIP** *quickly*
grabs **CANDY** *hostage.)*

PHILLIP. Nobody move or I'll kill her.

*(***BRENT** *sees the audience and gets back into character.)*

ALEXANDER. Like you killed all the others?

PHILLIP. That's right. It's true!

VICTOR. Why, Phillip? Why?

PHILLIP. I did it for you.

(to audience)

And you. The others were ruining everything.

ALEXANDER. And you cleverly faked your own death to
throw us off the track long enough for the show to
end.

PHILLIP. That's right. Now, get your hands up! All of you!

(All put their hands up.)

I had to kill them all. Don't you see? Hal Holst, that piss-poor actor. He mumbled so badly no one could understand a word he said. He asked to be killed. Admit it. You all wanted him dead.

(All mumble agreement and look away.)

And Banks...he deserved it, too. No one talks to the director like that and lives. Plus he only gave me thirty-five dollars to build a set. Do you know how much paint costs? Alabama Miller? No great loss there. He insisted you do the play the way he wrote it. Who does he think he is? Aaron Sorkin? He had to die. And old bag Crawford? Do I even need to go into it?

ALL. No.

CANDY. Somebody do something!

MONA. The lights!

*(**BRENT** dives at the light switch – which is painted on the wall. The lights stay on. **BRENT** looks foolish.)*

PHILLIP. Nice try, moron. Now, nobody move or the little lady buys the big one!

*(**PHILLIP** takes **CANDY** hostage and exits backstage as he speaks. He ends up backstage outside the window. **CHAZ** wakes up and sees **CANDY** at gunpoint.)*

CHAZ. Candy!

*(**CHAZ** quietly crawls offstage, as the others stand with their hands over their heads.)*

PHILLIP. None of you realize who you're working with. He is Victor Le Pewe. "Amarillo Galileo." Wonder Child of the Broadway Stage. Nobody treats him like this. Genius is never recognized in its own time. Why is that? Why? I saw it. I devoted my life to getting him back on top. Admired by millions. The world will someday see. Then you'll be sorry. Then you'll see why I had to do what I did. To save the show... It was all up to me...

(CHAZ yanks on the snow machine rope and a ton of snow is dumped on PHILLIP, who is knocked out of view. CANDY is rescued by CHAZ, as DICK runs offstage to capture PHILLIP.)

(as he is crushed by the snow)

Ahh!!

(ALEXANDER quickly crosses Down Stage Center.)

ALEXANDER. Looks like…snow…

(CHAZ and CANDY enter.)

BETTE. Good going, Drools.

PENELOPE. Oh, Drools, weren't you frightened?

DROOLS. Just a little.

(CHAZ faints dead away. DICK enters, handcuffed to PHILLIP.)

VICTOR. Poor Phillip. Blinded by love and artistic genius. Do you think the police will go lightly on him, Inspector?

DICK. Are you kidding? He's a homicidal maniac who just brutally murdered four innocent people.

VICTOR. But one was a producer and one was a playwright. Surely those two don't really count.

BETTE. Do you mean to say you really are a policeman, Inspector?

DICK. Yes, Miss Bette. Dick Scorsese, NYPD. I've been investigating the murder of piss-poor actor Hal Holst. By going undercover here as Inspector Mounds, I was able to spy on each and every one of you. We knew sooner or later someone would murder again. And this time, we were ready. So…now…my search has ended.

VICTOR. And we can go on with our lives!

PENELOPE. Oh, Alexander. Hold me. Hold me.

ALEXANDER. The snow…is melting at last!

(Sound effects: Music Builds To Crescendo)

(All pose dramatically.)

(Lights blackout)

(Applause and "bravos" are heard over the music.)

(Curtain call)

(Music: Dramatic Beethoven Finale.)

*(Lights up: Seated on the love seat are **ALABAMA MILLER**, **CONSTANCE CRAWFORD** and **PIGGY BANKS**. All are dead – eyes closed, holding lilies. **VICTOR LE PEWE** tilts each person's head forward for their bow, holding his other hand over their heads. After the three dead people bow, **VICTOR** runs offstage. **CANDY** and **CHAZ** enter together and bow. Next, **DICK SCORSESE** – handcuffed to **PHILLIP** – enters. They bow together. Next, **VICTOR LE PEWE** enters with a bouquet of roses, blowing kisses to everyone, including **PHILLIP** who gave him the roses. Finally, **MONA** and **BRENT** enter together, meeting at Center Stage, overdoing their love for one another. They bow together. ALL LIVE ACTORS join hands for a COMPANY BOW. The LIVE ACTORS then separate and motion to the DEAD ACTORS on the sofa. The DEAD ACTORS just sit there, dead. The LIVE ACTORS join hands for a COMPANY BOW.)*

(Curtain falls)

End of Play

COSTUME PLOT

CHAZ LOONEY/DROOLS – Black cutaway, white shirt, black tux pants, black shoes, black bow tie, white gloves. (into) Same with beret.

CANDY APPLES/PENELOPE – Ingenue dress with lace, overcoat, with black stockings and corset underneath, black heels.

BRENT REYNOLDS/ALEXANDER – White shirt, dark pants, colorful satin smoking jacket and ascot, red socks, dark shoes, overcoat, fedora.

DICK SCORSESE/INSPECTOR MOUNDS – Deerstalker coat and hat, black shoes, white shirt, tweed jacket, bow-tie, Martin Scorsese-look-alike glass frames.

MONA MONET/BETTE – Red Bette Davis/Joan Crawford type dress with shoulder pads, heels, long cigarette holder.

CONSTANCE CRAWFORD/LADY BARRINGTON – Long black skirt with white victorian blouse, cameo, red bloomers, black character shoes, grey Gibson Girl wog

VICTOR LE PEWE – Black jeans, grey t-shirt, open dress shirt, black boots.

P.G. "PIGGY" BANKS – Sharp blue suit, bling. (into) Same, with blood stained shirt and protruding scissors.

PHILLIP – Black t-shirt, black jeans, sneakers, black bedazzled "Phillip" toolbelt, scarf at neck.

ALABAMA MILLER – Rumpled tan pants, plaid shirt, old cardigan sweater, brown shoes, glasses.

"DROP DEAD!" PROP LIST

Cigarette holder

Serving tray

Clipboard

Magnifying glass

Large barrel revolver (Cap gun)

Small cap gun

Police revolver and shoulder strap

Starter pistol and caps

Blood capsules (small)

Surgical tape

Police Gazette

Pill bottle

2 pair scissors – one with attachment

6 "opening night" carnations

Police handcuffs

"Penelope" sign (Alabama)

Children's xylophone (doorbell)

Martin Scorsese glass frames

Flask (Alabama)

Big rubber knife

Overnight case (Penelope)

Old fashioned telephone

Large bulky headset

Small rubber ear piece

Telephone ringer box

Metal goblet

Straw

Plastic pail/shovel

Packing peanuts (for snow)

Roll of duct tape

Sand bag

Fireplace logs with light bulb

Music stand

Matching wigs (Crawford and Victor)

Compact (Chaz)

Letter

Bra

Fireplace poker and shovel

3 long-stemmed lilies (curtain call)

Tongue depressors (Brent)

ALSO BY BILLY VAN ZANDT & JANE MILMORE

Bathroom Humor

Confessions Of A Dirty Blonde

Do Not Disturb

Having A Wonderful Time, Wish You Were Her!

High School Reunion: The Musical

Infidelities!

Lie, Cheat, And Genuflect

A Little Quickie

Love, Sex, And The I.R.S.

Merrily We Dance And Sing (Musical)

A Night At The Nutcracker (Musical)

The Pennies (Musical)

Playing Doctor

The Senator Wore Pantyhose

Silent Laughter

Suitehearts

Till Death Do Us Part

What The Bellhop Saw

What The Rabbi Saw

Wrong Window!

You've Got Hate Mail

ALSO BY BILLY VAN ZANDT

The Property Known As Garland

Please consult samuelfrench.com for further licesning information or visit the authors' website at atvanzandtmilmore.com.